The Valley of
Lost Herds

The Valley of Lost Herds

W.C. Tuttle

Originally published in the May 15, 1927 issue of *Adventure*

Published by Wildside Press, LLC.
Visit us online at wildsidepress.com.

The Valley of Lost Herds

The big Tomahawk—saloon, gambling palace, honkatonk—blazed with lights. Cowboys jostled each other at the long bar, or laughed and made merry with the girls who thronged the rooms. The roulette whirred, poker chips rattled and the voices of the dealers droned above the roar of the crowd.

It was the big night of the month in Tomahawk—pay night on the Reber ranches. And pay night on the Reber ranches meant that all the small ranches to the north would also pay off and let their men come to town. There was no limit to anything. Reber owned the Tomahawk Saloon; owned nearly everything else in the town of Tomahawk, as far as that was concerned.

And with one exception he owned all of Reber Valley. It had been known as Tomahawk Valley, and was still Tomahawk Valley on the map, but to those who lived there it was Reber Valley. For Park Reber owned the M 33, Half-Wheel, Circle S, Two Bar X and the Lightning. There was really only one ranch he did not own, the S\ Bar\ P. There was another little place twenty miles south of Tomahawk which belonged to Jack Silver, who had never registered any brand. So, outside of the S\ Bar\ P, Park Reber really owned the valley.

In an area thirty miles long by about fifteen miles in width Park Reber was supreme—a real cattle baron. And Park Reber sat in his big house in Tomahawk town, all alone except for a Chinese cook, and gloated. He was *the* big man of the country—big and lonesome. And sometimes he was mad, they said. Men worked for him, spent their money in his saloon and gambling house; but none of them admired him.

He was about sixty years of age—white-haired, harsh of feature, his deep-set eyes gloomy. Over his left eye was a white scar like a crescent moon, and he often touched it, as if it annoyed him. He drove his men hard, demanded results and got most of their wages back *via* the green cloth.

It had taken him twenty years to become owner of the valley.
His herds, the Diamond R brand, roamed the many hills. While his ranches were all designated by their original brand names, all the stock was branded with the Diamond R. Other ranches shipped from Tomahawk, but the Diamond R was the heavy shipper. They owned the loading corrals—or rather Reber did.

Park Reber did not come often to the Tomahawk Saloon, but he had been coming oftener of late. Some said it was because of June Meline, the tall, black-haired beauty who played the violin. She was not a fiddler. There seemed a difference between June Meline and the rest of the girls of the honkatonk. Her white skin was untouched by rouge or paint and there was an imperious lift to her well shaped head. Nor did she mix with the others.

Park Reber loved music and most of all he loved the wailing notes of her violin. Often she had come to his table to talk with him. She refused drinks, but liked to discuss with him his business troubles. Some said she was trying to "rope-in" the old man, but Park Reber knew better. He admired her level-headed way of looking at things.

And on this pay night Park Reber came again, taking his usual table, where he might drink and watch the show. With him was "Slim" Patterson, foreman of the Half-Wheel ranch. Their table was near the platform, where the three-piece orchestra rattled out its tin-panny music.

The show was just at its height as they sat down. There was a burst of applause as June Meline came out carrying her violin. She was dressed in black silk, which accentuated the pallor of her skin. Only the piano played her accompaniment, and as she lifted her violin the pianist hesitated.

Some one had spoken a word aloud—the name of a man.

"'Buck' Priest!"

And there he stood, not more than six feet away from Park Reber, backed by two of his men. It was the first time Buck Priest had ever been in the Tomahawk Saloon. He was as old as Park Reber, possibly older. He wore his hair long, but his thin, evil face, with the hawk-bill nose, was smooth-shaven. He wore a silver-trimmed sombrero, buckskin shirt, gray trousers tucked in the tops of his high-heeled boots, and around his waist was a wide, beautifully carved leather cartridge belt supporting a holstered Colt.

The men with him were hard-bitted cowboys—fighting men of the S\ Bar\ P. It took nerve for Buck Priest to lead his men in among the cowboys of the Diamond R. But Buck Priest had nerve. He had fought Park Reber until Reber had told his men to leave the S\ Bar\ P alone.

At one time—over twenty years ago—these two men had been comrades.

It was evident that Buck Priest was drunk this night. He was not a drinking man, but once a year Buck Priest would get drunk; and when he got drunk, he was so cold-blooded that even his own men did not wish to associate with him.

It seemed as if every man in the room were holding his breath. Park Reber got slowly to his feet, and Priest laughed harshly.

"You dirty old cow thief!"

Buck Priest fairly hissed the words at Reber.

"You sneakin' old rustler!"

No one moved; no one spoke. The two men, one on each side of Buck Priest, were bent forward tensely, their eyes sweeping the room, ready to draw and shoot at the first move. Park Reber's eyes blinked angrily, but he held still, staring at Buck Priest.

"I'm talkin' to you, Reber," said Priest slowly. "Callin' you a thief. And you ain't gut guts enough to deny it. You've rustled my cows just as long as you're goin' to, Reber. I've come into the lion's den to tell yuh what I think of yuh, you cow thief!"

There could be but one answer to that accusation. Reber had been a gun-man, but of late years he had left that distinction to his hired men. He did not wear a belt and gun, but under his left arm-pit was a holstered Colt; and now he jerked back, reaching for this concealed gun.

It was what Buck Priest wanted, what he came there to force Park Reber to do—reach for a gun. His hand streaked down to his thigh and whipped up a big black-handled revolver. For a fraction of a second Park Reber's life was not worth a penny. Something flashed between Reber and Priest just as Priest pulled the trigger—something that smashed against Priest's hand and arm, partly ruining the shot which was intended for Park Reber's heart.

The big gun thundered as Buck Priest jerked sidewise. Park Reber stepped backward against his chair, tripped and fell to the floor. Priest and his two men whirled and headed for the doorway, and the crowd gave them plenty of room.

Men lifted Reber to his feet and then set him in a chair.

"That fiddler girl!" exclaimed one of them. "She threw her fiddle and hit Buck Priest on the arm."

The girl sprang from the platform and was at Park Reber's side in a moment, and he smiled at her. Slim Patterson ripped away the shoulder of his coat. The room was in an uproar. No one thought of going after Buck Priest. Some one went after a doctor, who came in a few minutes.

The bullet had struck high in Reber's shoulder, and he was quite ill. The doctor, skilled in gunshot cases, told him he was very lucky. Some one had recovered the violin, but it had been walked on until it hardly resembled an instrument. The girl looked ruefully at it, but said nothing.

Several of the cowboys secured a cot, using it in lieu of a stretcher, and carried Reber home; but not until he had received June Meline's assurance that she would act as his nurse.

"I wish you would," said the doctor. "Nurses are hard to find out here. And, anyway, your violin is broken."

"I'll buy yuh a carload," said Reber weakly. "Don't leave me alone with Hop Lee and this darned doctor. I've got lots of room up there, June."

And so June Meline became nurse for Park Reber. She knew little about nursing and told Park Reber so. But he grinned painfully and told her he didn't know much about being shot, as far as that was concerned.

She took up her residence in the big old house, which was really a ranchhouse, in the town. Hop Lee, the old Chinese cook, who cared for no one except Park Reber, took to June and actually smiled at her.

It was a new sensation to Park Reber, this idea of having a woman around. Not in nearly twenty-five years had he seen a woman in his house. His five foremen came at irregular intervals to report to him, and June often heard the name of Buck Priest spoken.

There was another name that caused Park Reber to curse—the name of Jack Silver.

It seemed that Jack Silver's name was connected with the word "rustler." There were two of these foreman that June did not like—Nort Jackson of the Lightning and Dave McLeese of the Two Bar X.

Nort Jackson was tall, thin, swarthy, black of eye, and wore a weak black mustache. He smiled at her too much, June thought. McLeese was ruddy of skin, with cold blue eyes under huge blonde brows. His nose had been broken across the arch and a huge scar twisted his mouth into a leer. Reber told her McLeese had been kicked in the face by a shod horse.

* * * *

It was several days after the shooting of Reber. Up to this time he had not mentioned Buck Priest to her. The doctor had finished dressing the wound and had given her orders for the feeding of the patient. Reber had been watching her closely for quite a while.

"Gettin' tired of bein' nurse to an old man?" he asked suddenly.

June smiled at him and shook her head.

"No, I'm not tired, Mr. Reber."

"That's good. I like you, June. You saved my life that night. Buck Priest is a good shot. He meant to kill me, yuh see. You shore thought real quick, June. You've got a head, girl. I've watched yuh around here and I've talked to yuh. You've got sense—too much sense to be playing a violin in a honkatonk."

June smiled at him.

"One must eat, Mr. Reber. And you have paid me better than I could get any other place."

"You've earned it, June. I wondered how they'd take yore kind of music. But cowboys are sentimental. I've seen 'em cry over yore music. Give the average cowboy a few drinks and he'll cry over 'Home Sweet

Home'. Yes, they will, June. Lot's of 'em never had a regular home; lots of 'em were kicked out early in life—but they'll cry, just the same."

"I suppose," said June, nodding.

"And you never asked me anythin' about Buck Priest. That night he called me a dirty cow thief, didn't he?"

Park Reber smiled bitterly.

"Mebbe Buck was drunk. He's hated me for years, June. Oh, I'm no angel. I tried to run Buck out of this country. He's a fighter. He's not sorry he shot me, but sorry he didn't kill me."

"Why didn't you have him arrested, Mr. Reber?"

"Arrested? For shootin' me? Why, no, June, it was an even break. My shoulder-holster—well, it isn't a fast draw. I'd have killed him. Oh, he hates me! Funny, isn't it, June? We used to be pardners—me and Buck.

"And it was all over a woman—a woman like you, June. She was like you in lots of ways, I think. The valley wasn't what it is now. Tomahawk was a tradin' post. This girl came here with her family in a covered wagon. I was in the south end of the valley at that time, where me and Buck had a small herd of cattle. Buck was here at the post, and met her.

"He was two days late bringing in supplies, and when he came he told me about her. I told him he was a fool to even think of a girl. It was a bad country to bring a girl into. The Cheyennes were unfriendly then, and there were a lot of them in the valley. They stole cattle and horses. It kept us busy protectin' our herds.

"But Buck went back to the post, over thirty miles from our ranch, and was gone five days. He was going to bring in more ammunition, but when he came back he was drunk and had no ammunition, so I left him there and went after it.

"And I met this girl. Her name was Janice Gray. Pretty name, eh? And she was pretty. I found that Buck had proposed to her and she had turned him down. Two days later we were married and went back to the ranch."

Park Reber smiled bitterly and looked at the ceiling.

"I don't know why she married me, June. I can see the look on Buck's face yet when we rode in and told him. And I had forgotten the ammunition. He didn't say much. Didn't wish us happiness—just sat there and looked at the ground. Finally he said—

"'Park, I'll pay you for this some day.'"

"I didn't know what he meant at the time. He saddled his horse and rode away. Later on he built a cabin at the forks of the river and sent two men for half of the stock. I helped them round up all the cattle and horses, and we divided them equally.

"But he never came near me. I heard that he said he would pay me back for what I had done, but I did not pay any attention to what I heard.

We were happy, Janice and I. The spring came and turned into summer. There were few settlers. The Cheyennes were gettin' worse, but every one said that when the winter came they'd be driven out by the deep snows and lack of game. The deer all move over to Clear Valley in the winter, because of the laurel, which does not grow here.

"The winter came early that season. I had cut a lot of wild hay on the bottoms, but not enough to feed stock all winter. In October there was three feet of snow, and it did not go off. By Christmas my hay was all gone, and I was in a desperate condition.

"I knew that the north end of the valley was open, and there was only one thing to try and do—to take my herd out of my range. I had one man working for me. He was a young man by the name of Sneed—John Sneed—a good boy. I couldn't leave Janice alone, yuh see. There would be a baby along soon, and some one had to stay with her. There was a doctor at the trading post. I tell yuh, I was desperate, so I broke trail with horses and led my cattle to the upper end of the valley. It was a tough pull. I took them past Buck's place, but didn't see him. He had moved his cattle out a few days before, and the trail was open from there.

"I had to bring those half-starved cattle almost up to here, where I threw them in with Buck's cattle, and came on to the post. It was bitter cold that night I rode in, but it warmed up a little, and by morning the worst blizzard that ever swept this country came down through here.

"This whole valley was a howling hell of wind and snow, June. I don't suppose our cattle lasted one night. You couldn't see a man at your elbow. A man couldn't live in it. Twenty below and a fifty-mile gale. I swore I'd go home, but they stopped me. It lasted five days.

"And when the wind died down the temperature died with it, until the thermometer at the post froze. Then we started for my place, the doctor and me, traveling on snowshoes. The valley was a place of the dead. There was not even a rabbit-track. Our cattle were under the drifts.

"There was some one at Buck's cabin. We could see a thread of smoke from his chimney; the rest of the cabin was buried in the snow. But there was no smoke from my chimney."

Park Reber shut his eyes, and for a while June thought he had fallen asleep. Then:

"No, there was no smoke, June; the cabin was empty. We dug our way down to the door and went in. There was John Sneed, lying face down in the middle of the room—dead. His head had been cut open—his scalp taken. The Cheyennes had been there. The doctor said he had been dead quite a while. I think they had been there ahead of the blizzard.

"I don't remember just what I did, June. They told me that I went hunting for the Cheyenne camp; I don't remember. Later I went back to the post and spent the winter. In the spring I went to the Cheyennes and tried to find some trace of my wife, but it was useless. They treated me like a crazy man—and I reckon I was. Later on I went further north and opened a saloon in a new mining camp. It was a money-maker, and in two years I came back here and went into cattle again.

"Buck was still here; still hatin' me. We met one day and he taunted me with my loss. I tried to kill him with my hands and almost succeeded. It didn't help any. Buck Priest ain't the kind you can whip into friendship.

"And I think he hates me for being successful. I own practically all of the Valley. They call it Reber's Valley. That must hurt Buck Priest. I tried to buy him out, but he wouldn't sell. He shot my cattle when they came on his range, and I—I shot his cattle on my range.

"Oh, it's been a battle for years. Finally I gave my men orders to let him and his cattle alone. It seemed to be a mutual truce. But my cattle have disappeared. I don't think Buck Priest took them."

"Who is Jack Silver?" asked June.

Reber looked curiously at her.

"Jack Silver?"

"Yes, I heard his name spoken, Mr. Reber."

"Jack Silver," mused Reber. "A handsome devil of a breed, June. He's tall, graceful—too smart for my men. He comes to Tomahawk. He's not afraid of me. Half Cheyenne. There are no Cheyennes in the Valley now, June. Uncle Sam keeps 'em on a reservation. But Jack Silver lives back on Trapper Creek, twenty miles southwest of here. We've tried to catch him stealing my cattle, but he eludes us.

"McLeese of the Two Bar X and Nort Jackson of the Lightnin' have trailed him for weeks; and Slim Patterson has tried to trap him, but he's too clever. He's got the cunning of the Cheyenne, the brain of a white man."

June sat in an old rocker, her chin resting on the palm of her right hand, as she thought over Reber's story. It was the first time she had ever heard the reasons for Buck Priest's hatred of Park Reber.

"How many head of cattle has Jack Silver stolen from you?" she asked.

Reber shook his head slowly.

"Who knows, June? More than I care to lose."

He smiled at the thoughtful expression on her face.

"What would you do if you was in my place, June?"

"I was just thinking," said June, "that if I were in your place I'd hire Jack Silver to work for me."

Reber frowned quickly. "Hire him to—"

"Why not? You'd save money—and he would be worth what you paid him, wouldn't he?"

"I never thought of that, June."

They were interrupted by Hop Lee, who came in and told Reber that Slim Patterson of the Half-Wheel was waiting to see him. June left the room when Patterson came in.

"How're yuh comin'?" asked Slim, sitting down in the chair June had vacated.

"All right," said Reber. "Be out in a day or so."

"Good! Say, I was back between Trapper Creek and the West Fork yesterday and I found about a hundred cows bunched in a draw back there. It shore looked as though somebody was all set for a drive. Me and 'Chuck' Avery laid there until night waitin' for somebody to show up, but they didn't.

"I left Chuck there and went home. Sent 'Biddy' Conley and Abe Lehman out to keep him company and pulled out for here this mornin', after Biddy came in and said they hadn't seen anybody yet."

Reber sighed wearily.

"I dunno, Slim," he said slowly. "I talked with McLeese the other day and he suggested that we post men in that Trapper Creek pass. It might be a good scheme. They can't get past the Two Bar X into West Fork pass without bein' seen by some of the boys, and those are the only two ways out, except past here.

"I'll tell yuh what I want yuh to do, Slim. Send about three of yore men to Trapper Creek pass, and then pack a message to Jackson, McLeese, Franks and Carlin to be here at my place tomorrow night, and you come with 'em. I've got a scheme to stop Jack Silver."

"You have? That's fine."

Slim got to his feet and picked up his hat.

"I'll pass the word to the boys for tomorrow night. Heard anythin' more of Buck Priest?"

"Not a word, Slim. Have you?"

"Only that he says yo're stealin' his cows. I think he's tryin' to excuse himself for shootin' yuh."

Reber smiled slowly, and Slim went out.

* * * *

The S\ Bar\ P ranchhouse and other buildings were of log construction, rambling old structures one story in height. The ranchhouse and bunkhouse had the old mud-and-stone fire-places. Back of the stables was Porcupine Creek, which ran northwest to Tomahawk River. It was about six miles from the ranch to Tomahawk town.

It was the day after Reber had sent the message to his foremen when Jack Silver rode in at the S\ Bar\ P ranch. He rode a tall black gelding, a fitting mount for a man of his physique.

Silver was tall, lithe, dark-skinned. He wore his hair long, but his face was smooth-shaven. His shirt was black, as were his muffler and sombrero, and he wore no chaps. His high-heeled boots were of the short-topped Southwest style, and around his waist was a hand-made cartridge belt supporting a Colt gun in a hand-made holster.

He swung off his horse, waving a greeting to three of Buck Priest's men who were down near the corrals. Priest met him at the door of the ranchhouse and they shook hands warmly.

"How are yuh, Jack?" asked Priest, as they sat down in the main room of the ranchhouse.

"I'm fine," replied Silver. "Been over in Clear Valley for a week and just got back. Ran into Dave McLeese yesterday and he told me about you and Reber havin' a fight."

Priest scowled heavily and slapped the palm of his right hand on his knee.

"I tried to kill him, Jack. A girl ruined the shot."

Silver smiled, showing a flash of white, even teeth.

"A girl, eh? McLeese didn't tell me about her."

"A fiddler in the Tomahawk," said Priest. "Flung her fiddle and hit me in the hand. Oh, I was goin' to kill him, Jack. Reber and his gang of cutthroats are runnin' all the S\ Bar\ P cattle out of the valley."

"I thought there was sort of a truce."

"Truce!" Priest laughed shortly. "Reber sent me word that he'd quit if I would. I quit, Jack. But he didn't. The only way I can ever make Park Reber quit is to kill him. Next time there won't be any fiddle-throwin' female present."

Jack Silver laughed softly.

"You know what they think of me, Buck. I'm watched every minute by Reber's men. Why, I can't even kill a piece of fresh meat any more. They're layin' for a chance to kill me. Some day they'll put up a job on me—and I'll swing for it.

"Oh, they're nice to my face—McLeese, Jim Carlin, Nort Jackson—all nice to my face. Behind my back they call me the dirty half-breed—the Injun rustler. I trap for a livin', Buck. You know that. Reber hates me because I'm half Cheyenne."

Buck Priest smiled crookedly, nodding slowly.

"There's plenty of hate in this valley, Jack. I hope some day to see Park Reber suffer."

"He ought to be half Injun," said Silver bitterly. "That's enough sufferin' for one man. Last night he sent word to me by one of the Half-Wheel punchers to be at his place tonight."

"He sent word to you?"

"Yeah."

"Wants to trap yuh, eh?"

Silver shrugged his shoulders.

"I played safe, Buck. Today I came across the hills and I'll stay here until dark. I don't know what Reber wants."

"He's still crippled, and that girl is nursin' him. She's makin' a play for Reber."

"Pretty girl, Buck?"

Priest nodded.

"Yeah, pretty as a picture. But what do yuh suppose Reber wants of you?"

"I dunno."

"Are you goin' to take a chance on him, Jack?"

"I'll see what he wants."

"It might be a scheme to harm yuh, Jack."

"Might be. But as far as that's concerned, if they want to kill me they can pick me off most any time."

"That's true," agreed Priest. "We'll all ride in after supper, Jack. If things go wrong, we'll do what we can."

"And if Reber finds you in town he'll set his dogs on yuh," said Silver grimly.

"I'll have my dogs along," replied Buck meaningly. "We went into the Tomahawk and came out safe enough. But I was drunk, Jack. It wasn't a job for a sober man. We sure shocked that gang a-plenty."

"I wish I had been there," smiled Jack. "I've never been in the Tomahawk."

"It's not a safe place, Jack; and maybe you'll find it out tonight."

* * * *

None of Reber's foremen knew why he had sent for them. Some of them were obliged to ride the length of the valley, but they were all there—Patterson, Jackson, McLeese, Carlin and Franks. McLeese was drunk; not blind drunk by any manner of means, but inclined to be quarrelsome.

Park Reber was out of bed, and met them in the big living-room, a huge place forty feet long and twenty-five feet wide. Around two sides of this huge room was a wide veranda. At one end was a doorway leading out on to the veranda; and there was another doorway about fifteen feet from the corner, on the side. About midway of the room was a big window, and there were two windows at the front end.

Across this front end of the room was a long table and a number of chairs. On the opposite side of the room from the side entrance was a huge fireplace, capable of taking ten-foot logs. Most of the furnishings were of the home-made variety, and the floors were strewn with bright-colored Navajo rugs and the skins of wolf and grizzly. The walls were darkened with smoke and age.

The five foremen came in together. Reber seated them around the big table, he himself sitting at the head of the table, still a trifle pale, unable to use his left arm. At his right sat June Meline. She received several undisguised scowls. Beside her sat Franks of the M 33. At the opposite end of the table sat McLeese, scowling at everybody, and June in particular. He did not like the idea of having a woman at their conference. On the other side of the table sat Patterson, Jackson and Carlin.

Reber's glance swept around the table and came to rest on McLeese.

"You're drunk," he said shortly. "Why?"

McLeese grimaced and tried to laugh it off, but Reber's eyes bored into him and he coughed a little.

"I wanted sober men at this meetin'," said Reber.

"I'm sober enough to know what I'm doin'," said McLeese.

"Not if you had three drinks—and you've had more."

Reber did not wait for McLeese to reply, but turned to the others.

"I brought you boys here tonight to see if we can't figure out some way to stop this rustlin'," he said slowly. "We're losin' too many cattle to suit me. What's to be done?"

Patterson shook his head.

"I dunno, Park," he said slowly. "It beats me."

"How about you, Jackson?"

"Same as Slim."

"Same here," growled Carlin.

"They ain't hit my place," said Franks of the M 33. "Mebbe I'm too far north."

"That may be," nodded Reber. "But it's got to stop."

"Go out and stop old Buck Priest," said McLeese.

Reber studied McLeese's flushed face.

"You think they're runnin' 'em out this end of the valley, Mac?"

"Priest hates yuh, don't he? They're not goin' over the West Fork pass, and the boys have been watchin' the Trapper Creek pass. Jack Silver is friendly to Buck Priest. By ——, I'd wipe out that whole —— gang."

"There's a lady present," said Reber coldly.

"I forgot," said McLeese. "Anyway, I don't think this is any place for a woman."

"I asked her to be here," said Reber. "When I want yore opinion on that I'll ask for it, McLeese!"

"I'm jist wonderin' if McLeese's idea ain't worth quite a lot, at that," said Jackson. "I don't mean about the lady, but about Priest and Silver. We've tried to trap Silver a lot of times, but he's too much Injun to be trapped."

"He's smart," said McLeese.

"Too smart for you, eh?" asked Reber.

"Oh, I dunno," flared McLeese.

"You haven't landed him, and that's the answer," said Reber. "He's too smart. He thinks twice while you're thinkin' once. And you object to this lady being here. She's got more sense in a minute than you'll ever show, McLeese."

Both June and McLeese flushed, but for different reasons.

The rest of the men eyed June closely. Perhaps they thought Reber was getting old and that this pretty girl was in a position to get a hand into the Reber fortune. It was an embarrassing position for the girl. McLeese laughed, and they saw Reber's lips tighten. Carlin kicked at McLeese's ankle beneath the table, but only succeeded in kicking a leg of the table.

"We're not gettin' anywhere," said Reber coldly.

"No, and we'll not get anywhere as long as you'll let Jack Silver and Buck Priest do as they please," growled Carlin. "Let's clean 'em out, I say."

"On what evidence, Carlin?"

"General principles. Buck tried to kill you. He'll try it again. Silver is a half-breed thief. Just pass the word and we'll rid the valley of the whole brood."

"Meanin'," said Reber slowly, "that Silver is too smart for you to catch red-handed, eh?"

"If yuh want to put it that way—yes."

"You think he bunches up cattle and takes 'em through the Trapper Creek pass and sells 'em in Clear Valley?"

"Cinch. We can't get any evidence in Clear Valley. We've tried it often enough."

"That gang over there will take stolen cattle, that's a cinch," said Jackson. "You'd never get any evidence if yuh went there in a gang—and one or two men would soon be wiped out. They're pretty clannish."

Reber nodded slowly. He knew Jackson was right. Suddenly there came the slither of a moving body, and they turned toward the big window about ten feet beyond them. Just inside the window stood Jack Silver, his left shoulder resting against the wall, his two thumbs hooked over his belt.

For several moments no one spoke. Silver laughed, and his teeth flashed white in the light from the hanging lamp in the center of the room. He seemed to be resting lazily against that shoulder, but every man at that table knew he could draw and shoot quicker than any of them.

"Gentlemen, Mr. Silver himself," said Reber slowly.

The men glanced at Reber curiously, but turned back to Silver.

"You sent for me," said Jack.

Reber nodded.

"Yeah, I sent for yuh, Silver. Slim, will you get a chair for Mr. Silver?"

Slim Patterson started to get up, but Silver halted him.

"I'll stand up," he said slowly, smiling again. "Since when did the Reber outfits start havin' squaws at their council?"

June straightened in her chair, her eyes flashing. Silver's laugh was almost an insult. Reber did not look at her. McLeese grinned in evident enjoyment.

"Silver," said Reber firmly, "you're deliberately tryin' to antagonize us, but I'll overlook it. I asked you here tonight to make you a proposition. Will you go to work for me as a foreman on one of my ranches?"

It was like a bomb-shell exploding in the room. The idea of offering Jack Silver a position as foreman! The men wondered whether Reber was losing his mind. Even Silver laughed.

"Make me a foreman?" said Silver. "What's the idea, Reber?"

"That's my business, Silver. I'm makin' you that offer."

Silver's eyes swept the faces of the five foremen.

"Which ranch?" he asked smiling.

"Any one you'll take."

Silver's amused glance came back to June.

"Which one is the squaw goin' to take?"

Reber shook his head sadly.

"You don't understand what I'm offerin' you, Silver."

"Yes, I do, Reber."

Silver was not smiling now and he had shoved away from the wall.

"You're tryin' to buy me off—tryin' to get me to work for you. You're afraid of me, Reber. I dunno why, but yuh are. Your men watch me day and night. I'm tired of it, but not so tired that I'll take a job with you. You hate me because I'm half Cheyenne.

"You ran my people out of Tomahawk Valley, Reber. I know your story—know why you hate my people. I had a little herd of cattle started, but you and your men killed 'em off to keep me from being a cattleman. I've no cause to love you. I don't want your job. Give it to the squaw."

17

He flung his left leg across the windowsill, and before any one could say anything further, he disappeared. Patterson sprang to his feet, and the other men were behind him, but Reber stopped them.

"Sit down," he ordered. "He's done no wrong."

"The dirty half-breed!" snarled McLeese.

June Meline was on her feet, her hands on the table, as she leaned forward, staring at the window where Silver had disappeared. He had taunted her, called her a squaw! But there was something romantically wild about this tall, slim, white-toothed young man who defied them. He had laughed at them and refused to work for Park Reber.

"The trouble is," Reber was speaking, "yo're all afraid of Jack Silver."

June turned quickly to Reber.

"I'm not," she declared.

Reber smiled at her.

"You're not, June?"

"Not a bit. I'll bet I could trap him."

Several of the men laughed aloud.

"He'd steal you," declared McLeese, and then laughed at his own statement.

"You think you could, eh?" said Reber slowly. "I wonder."

"Ridiculous," declared Jackson.

Reber leaned on the table looking at June, studying her keenly. Suddenly he struck the table with his clenched fist.

"I'll do it!" he exclaimed. "June, beginnin' tomorrow you'll be a ranch-foreman for the Diamond R."

He looked around at the hard-bitted faces of his men, who were looking at him, wondering whether he was in his right mind.

"What ranch?" asked McLeese.

Reber shifted his eyes to McLeese.

"The Two Bar X."

McLeese's ranch. He shut his jaws tightly and looked at Reber. He knew it meant that Reber was going to fire him.

"That's a —— of a note!" he snorted.

"I run my ranches to suit myself, McLeese."

Reber reached in his pocket and took out a wallet, from which he counted out several bills. He handed them to McLeese.

"That's yore pay up to the first of the month, McLeese."

"And I'm through right now, eh?"

"Yeah, right now."

"All right," McLeese got to his feet unsteadily. "I've got some personal stuff at the ranch and I'll go get it."

Reber nodded, and they watched McLeese leave the house. None of the other men made any comment. For several moments after McLeese was gone Reber stared silently at the door. Then:

"I think that's all boys. Goodnight."

He got to his feet and June walked from the room with him. The men looked curiously at him, and went out.

"I need a shot of liquor," said Patterson dryly. "Personally, I think the old man is losin' his mind."

"He's as crazy as a bedbug!" snapped Carlin. "Offers a job to Jack Silver, and then gives it to a —— woman! I'll take a drink with yuh."

* * * *

Park Reber wanted to go with June to the Two Bar X ranch the next day, but the old doctor vetoed such a move on the part of his patient. Reber was far from well. There was none of his men in from the ranches, so he sent Jud Nelson and Sam Heard, two of his men who worked in Tomahawk, to accompany June.

These men did not know why June was going to the ranch, nor did they ask Reber. They loaded June and her baggage into a light wagon, kicked off the brake and drove out of town. It was nearly thirty miles to the Two Bar X, and the roads were none too good. June occupied the back seat, and with the rattle and lurch of the vehicle there was little opportunity for conversation. The two men devoted themselves exclusively to chewing tobacco and keeping the wagon on the road.

At the forks of the river, about twelve miles south of town, they saw Slim Patterson and two of his cowboys. The road passed close to the Half-Wheel ranchhouse. Slim waved at them, but they did not stop. They took the right-hand road, which led to the Two Bar X. There were no bridges, and the river crossings were almost deep enough to float the wagon.

About three miles south of the Half-Wheel ranch they passed the mouth of Trapper Creek, One of the men told her it was Trapper Creek, and she knew that Jack Silver's place was somewhere between the West Fork and the mountains.

June was still in somewhat of a daze over her new job. She didn't know a thing about cattle; she knew nothing about running a ranch. But Reber had told her merely to use her head. He was the real head of all the ranches, and he would see that she learned the game. Not that Reber intended keeping her at the Two Bar X. He was not crazy. But he was willing to grasp at any straw to stop the cattle rustling. If June could figure out a way to trap Silver it would be worth many dollars to the Diamond R and he was going to give her a chance.

19

He knew the temper of his men, knew that the majority of them were against the idea of hiring a woman. But he did feel that any of them would support any scheme she might formulate to stop the wholesale stealing of his cattle.

They had just passed the mouth of Trapper Creek and were traveling through a willow patch in the river bottom, near a ford, when the driver suddenly jerked up his team, almost throwing June off the seat. She had a confused impression of the team's twisting sidewise, of a man yelling a warning, of the sound of a shot.

She flung out her right hand, grasping the back of the front seat to steady herself. Sam Herd was sprawling forward, as if looking down over the left front wheel, and he suddenly slid ahead limply and slithered over the wheel to the ground.

Jud Nelson's two hands were in the air. Two masked men had turned their horses in close to the wagon. They were wearing empty flour sacks over their heads, with holes cut in them for eyes. One of them looked down at Herd.

"That's one less for Reber," he growled behind his mask.

The one man kept a rifle trained on Nelson, while the other dismounted, climbed up and removed Nelson's revolver.

June's face was pale, but she kept her nerve when this masked man turned to her.

"Git out of the wagon," he ordered gruffly.

There was nothing else for her to do. These men had killed one man already. She climbed down and he indicated his horse.

"Climb on."

She looked at Nelson, who was looking straight ahead, his lips compressed tightly, both hands held rigidly above his head. June could ride. She climbed into the saddle, hampered by her skirts, and the other bandit laughed.

"Good lookin' squaw," he observed.

The other man turned and walked around the wagon to where Herd's body lay. He picked him up, carried him to the rear of the wagon and dumped him unceremoniously over the tailgate into the wagon-box. He came back and motioned to Nelson.

"Turn around and drive back," he said hoarsely. "Take all the time yuh need. A little hurry might ruin yore health."

"And yuh might tell old Reber that he ain't runnin' this valley yet a while," added the other. "The road from here to Tomahawk won't be healthy for him and his men, so they don't need to blame us if they git what this feller got."

Nelson nodded. He was more than willing to get away with a whole skin. He managed to turn the team around in the willows, and started back, holding the team to a slow walk.

The man mounted behind June, but before they started out he blindfolded her with a none too clean handkerchief.

Then they rode out of the river bottom, forded the river and headed into the hills. June knew this, because the horse was climbing most of the way. There was no conversation. The bandit guided the horse, with an arm on each side of June. He had been drinking, but not enough to give him more than a whisky breath.

It seemed to June that they had been riding about an hour, when the horses fairly slid downward for considerable distance, traveled along for a while on level ground and stopped. The men dismounted and lifted June off the saddle, guiding her into a cabin, where they removed the blindfold.

It was a small log cabin, crudely furnished, with a dirt floor. It smelled musty in there. June blinked painfully as she looked around at the two men. One of them secured a length of lariat-rope with which he roped her tightly to a chair. He knew how to knot ropes, and when he was finished there was no possible way for June to escape. The other man inspected the knots and nodded his approval.

"That's the old Injun knot," he growled. "No squaw ever wiggled loose from one like that."

The other laughed.

"You'll stay here quite a while," he told June. "No use to yelp. There ain't a man within miles of here. When Jack Silver does a job, he does it well. Park Reber can hunt and be —— to him, but he'll never find yuh. We're goin' away, but we'll be back tonight some time and bring some feed for yuh."

They turned abruptly and left the cabin, closing the door behind them. June heard the creak of their saddles and the sound of the horses walking away. She tried to loosen her bonds, but she soon found that there was nothing to do but to sit and wait.

She wanted to cry, to scream for help. But she knew that it would not help matters in the least. She was going to need all her nerve. She wondered what Park Reber would do. What could he do, she wondered? It might take them weeks to find her. Jack Silver had outwitted him again.

She wondered whether one of these men was Silver. Neither looked like the man who had taunted her. They were not so tall and slim as Silver.

It was, possibly, thirty minutes after the departure of the two men when she heard the soft *plop-plop* of a horse's hoofs. She listened intently. The horse had stopped near the cabin door, and she heard a footstep.

Suddenly the door was flung open and a man stood in the opening—a tall, slender man. She was looking against the light and could not see his features, but she knew it was Jack Silver.

He came slowly in and stood looking down at her.

"Reber's squaw, eh?" he said softly.

June shut her lips tightly, refusing to reply. He walked back to the door and looked around. Beyond him she could see his tall black horse looking toward him. Finally he came back to her and began taking off the ropes.

It did not take him long to unfasten her hands, and then he dropped to his knees beside her, fumbling with the knots beneath the chair. It was her big chance, and she had the nerve to take advantage of it.

Leaning slightly toward him she reached down and quickly whipped the six-shooter from his holster and shoved the muzzle against his neck. June knew guns. The hammer came to full cock from a twist of her thumb.

Jack Silver did not look up, but his hands came away from the rope. He did not move, but waited for her to act.

"Unfasten that rope," she ordered, and was surprized to find her voice fairly steady.

Silver unfastened the remaining rope, and she got to her feet, backing away from him.

"Now I've got you," she said hoarsely.

"Looks thataway," he said slowly. "I hope yuh know that trigger only pulls about a pound."

"I am not interested in trigger pulls, Mr. Silver."

"Possibly not. I am."

June picked up the loose rope with her left hand, keeping an eye on Silver, and then motioned for him to precede her out of the cabin. He made no objection, but his eyes were just a little curious.

June tossed him the looped end of the rope.

"Put it around your neck," she ordered.

He shut his lips tightly and studied her intently. She had the gun at her hip now, and the hammer was still cocked. He shrugged his shoulders and smiled thinly.

"Single-handed lynchin'?" he asked.

June shook her head firmly.

"I'm not your judge, Jack Silver. But you're going to guide me to the Two Bar X ranch, you know. You'll walk ahead with the rope around your neck and I'll ride your horse."

Jack Silver laughed softly as he put the loop around his neck.

"So that's your game, eh?" he said amusedly. "You've got a lot of nerve for a woman. I never knew that pretty women had nerve. That's how yuh won old man Reber, eh? Pretty girl with plenty nerve. Oh, he's worth winnin'. He's got nobody to leave his money to—no relatives. And he's got plenty money. I heard he had made you a foreman."

Silver threw back his head and laughed.

June had a notion to yank the loop tight and choke off that laugh.

"You'll laugh different when I get you to the Two Bar X," she promised him.

He sobered suddenly.

"That's right," he said quickly. "They don't like me. But what I'd like to know is what you were doing in this cabin all tied up like that?"

"How did you know I was in that cabin?" she retorted.

"I didn't. I saw two men riding away from here, so I came to investigate. Where most men are my enemies, I kinda look at things, yuh know."

"You lie!"

Silver's eyes narrowed with sudden anger.

"You know you lie," said June hotly. "You and your men knew I was going to the Two Bar X today. You had them stop us, and they killed a man—Sam Herd. You had them bring me to this place. That's how you knew I was here. Now I'm going to take you to the Two Bar X and turn you over to the men. You're responsible for the death of Sam Herd, and if Park Reber's men don't hang you the law will!"

Silver turned his head away and stared off across the hills.

"Your men won't be back for quite a while so you don't need to look for them," said June. "How far is it to the Two Bar X?"

"About three miles," said Silver slowly. "You better let the hammer down on that gun before yuh mount. Don't be afraid of that horse—he's gentle enough. Compadre! Stand still and let the squaw get on."

June managed to get into the saddle without tangling up the rope. She did not dare take her eyes off Silver, and she did not uncock the revolver. June was taking no chances.

"Now you take me straight to the Two Bar X ranch," she ordered, "and don't try any tricks."

"You are a very, very smart young lady," he said seriously. "And I am not going to try and trick yuh."

* * * *

About the time that June and Jack Silver were leaving for the Two Bar X ranch, a rider came through the gate of the S\ Bar\ P; a rider who swayed down along the fork of his saddle, a limp arm hanging on each side of the horse's neck.

The rider was Harry O'Steen, one of Buck Priest's men—a red-headed, freckled cowboy; a laughing, rollicking sort of person, whose disposition did much to keep up the morale of the S\ Bar\ P.

Buck Priest was sitting on the ranchhouse porch talking with "Rowdy" Dow, another of his cowboys, when the horse came in. They could see at a glance that O'Steen had been hurt, and both of them ran down to him. They eased him to the ground and then carried him to the shade of the porch.

"Been shot twice," declared Rowdy. "Gawd A'mighty, he's all shot to strings!"

Buck Priest nodded shortly and knelt beside O'Steen, who was trying to talk. Rowdy ran through the house and came back with a dipper of water, which he held to O'Steen's lips. Ken Mader and Dick Leeson, the two other cowboys, came from the bunk-house and joined them.

"Can yuh talk, Harry?" asked Buck anxiously. "Who shot yuh?"

O'Steen struggled painfully, trying to say something. It came in a jerky sentence—

"Rustlers—got—me—Porcupine—Creek—"

That was all. He closed his eyes, twitched slightly. Buck got to his feet, his old face twisted.

"Uh-huh," he said softly. "Rustlers got him on Porcupine Creek, boys. Help me carry him in the house. That's more of Park Reber's work."

They placed the body of O'Steen on a cot and covered it up with a bright-colored blanket.

"Saddle up," ordered Priest. "Take yore rifles along. We're goin' to Tomahawk and talk to Park Reber with the only language he understands. He's goin' to pay for killin' O'Steen."

"That's the talk," said Rowdy. "We'll wipe his town off the map."

"Four men may not be able to do that, Rowdy," said Buck Priest wearily, "but we'll do what we can."

Ten minutes later the four men galloped from the S\ Bar\ P, heading for Tomahawk town. The sun was almost down, and they wanted to get there before dark. About two miles from the ranch the road intersected with the main road, and as the four riders swept around the point of a hill they saw a team and light wagon coming from the south.

They were close enough to see that the driver was Nelson, one of Reber's men. They drew rein and waited for the wagon to reach them. Priest swung his horse across the road ahead of the team, forcing them to stop.

"Hyah, Nelson," said Priest coldly.

"Howdy, gentlemen," nodded Nelson. "I'm sure glad to see somebody. I stopped at the Half-Wheel, but there wasn't nobody at home. Me and

Sam Herd was takin' that girl to the Two Bar X and we got held up. Sam tried to draw a gun, and they killed him. And they put the girl on a horse and took her away. Sam's in the back of the wagon."

Rowdy spurred his horse around the wagon and looked in.

"He's here all right, Buck," he said.

"Where'd this all happen?"

"Near the mouth of Trapper. Down in them willers, jist before yuh reach the ford. Two men, Priest. They had sacks over their heads."

Priest backed his horse off the road and motioned for Nelson to drive on.

"Ain't we goin'?" asked Rowdy.

Buck Priest watched the wagon disappear up the road.

"I don't know what to make of it," he said. "Sam Herd was one of Park Reber's trusted men. And they stole that girl, eh? That's funny. We're goin' back home, boys. No use goin' off half-cocked, I reckon. We'll pack up some grub and blankets and swing in on the Porcupine. It must have been kinda late when O'Steen was shot, and the rustlers can't move cattle much after dark."

They turned and rode back to the ranch.

* * * *

In the meantime Nelson lost no time in driving his jaded horses to Tomahawk town. It was dark when he arrived, and he went straight to Reber's house, where he found Reber with the old doctor. Nelson blurted out his story as quickly as possible. He helped the doctor carry Herd's body into the house, and the doctor found that Herd had been killed almost instantly.

Reber, still weak from his wound, sat down in a chair and swore impotently.

"Just for that I'll wipe Buck Priest and Jack Silver off the map," he declared bitterly. "You say you met Priest and his men? They circled back to see if you got help at the Half-Wheel. Oh, I know Buck Priest!"

"Only one of 'em looked in at the body," said Nelson.

"They knew it was there. Oh, I'll make Priest pay. It was either Priest or Silver—perhaps both. They work together. Nelson, go to the Tomahawk and see if any of my men are in from the ranches. Bring them here to me. Wait! Send them here. You get a horse and ride for the Half-Wheel. Don't spare the horse. Tell Slim Patterson what happened. Then you go to the Circle S and tell Jim Carlin to bring his outfit to the Half-Wheel and to send a man to the Lightnin' for Jackson and his crew. We'll all meet at the Half-Wheel."

Nelson ran from the house, and the old doctor turned to Reber.

"You'll not ride tonight," he said firmly.

"You try to stop me, Doc."

"Hm-m-m-m! You're a fool, Park. That wound isn't healed up. You'll wreck your health, I tell you."

"Bah! Wreck my health! I'm goin' out to find that girl and to whip all this scum out of the valley. I've stood all I'll ever stand from Priest and Silver."

"It was a foolish thing, that sending of a woman," said the old doctor. He had known Park Reber for years, and felt privileged to speak his mind.

"Mebbe," said Reber shortly. "Mebbe not. She's smart, Doc. I wish she was my daughter. If things had turned out different I might have had a girl or a boy of about her age."

"Yes, that's true."

"And she spoiled Buck Priest's shot," said Reber. "He's got no love for her. I wonder where these men would take her? Not to any known place, that's a cinch. She's their ace in the hole. I'd like to get my two hands around Buck Priest's throat and choke the truth from him. Oh, he hates me, Doc!

"When he looks at me with his lop-sided grin, I feel that he's gloating over somethin'."

"Be calm," advised the doctor. "You'll work yourself into a fever. Did any doctor ever have such a patient to contend with? That meeting almost ruined everything; and now you insist on getting excited and riding helter-skelter over the hills in the dark! I ought to tie you down."

"Here come some of my men," said Reber. "Now you keep your tongue out of it, Doc. I'm goin', if I have to go on a stretcher."

* * * *

It was almost dark when Jack Silver led the way to the Two Bar X. There were no lights in the ranchhouse. June dismounted and forced Jack to knock on the door. But there was no answer to his knock. The door was unlocked. Without any orders from June, Jack lighted the big lamp in the main room.

"Where is everybody?" wondered June. "Is this the Two Bar X?"

"It's the Two Bar X all right," said Jack.

His heels were sore from the long walk in high-heeled boots and he limped painfully.

June pointed at a door across the room.

"Open that," she ordered.

Jack limped over and opened it.

It was a windowless inside room, evidently used as a bedroom by some one who cared little for ventilation. There was a small lamp on the table, and June ordered Jack to light it. She told him to remove the rope, and then she backed into the main room, closing the door behind her.

At some time the room must have been used for storage purposes, because there was a hasp and staple fastener. June quickly locked the door, after which she sat down in a chair and drew the first calm breath she had taken since Jack Silver had entered the deserted cabin. There was no way for him to get out of that room. She took a small lamp and went on a tour of investigation. The kitchen was fairly clean and there was plenty of food.

She cooked a meal for herself, but was afraid to take any of it to Silver. She had him under lock and intended keeping him. She felt sure that the men of the Two Bar X would be coming back soon. Perhaps, she thought, they heard of what happened to her and were searching for her.

And what a surprize it would be for them to come back and find her there, and to find Jack Silver a prisoner. She washed the dishes and went back to the main room. It was very quiet. A new moon was peeping over the crest of the Tomahawk range, and she heard the distant howling of a coyote.

She put Jack Silver's gun on the table beside her and sat down to look at some old magazines. Suddenly she heard the muffled tread of horses walking and thought it was the boys of the ranch coming home. She ran to a front window and looked out, but could see no one.

For several minutes she stood at the window, but the half-light was baffling. She went back and sat down, after deciding that it had been some loose horses. But something made her feel that she was being watched. Perhaps it was sort of sixth sense.

She found herself unable to read. The two dull, uncurtained windows seemed to stare at her like a pair of eyes. Why didn't they curtain their windows, she wondered? There were noises, too—queer noises.

Suddenly there came the scrape of leather sole on the porch, and the door was flung open. June jerked forward, her hand on the big gun.

Two men stepped inside, looking queerly at her. It was McLeese, the deposed foreman, and Chuck Bell, a big, raw-boned, square-faced cowboy who worked for the Two Bar X. McLeese glanced at the hand and gun on the table.

"Yuh got here, eh?" he said easily. "That's fine. I was kinda late gettin' here for my stuff. Where's all the boys?"

"I don't know," said June. "I haven't been here long."

"Uh-huh," nodded McLeese. "I suppose they're late gettin' in. Well, I'll gather up my stuff and head back for town. Did yuh come out alone?"

"Two men brought me," said June.

She didn't want to tell McLeese anything, because she didn't trust him.

"And went back and left yuh alone, eh? Dirty trick. This is a lonesome place for a girl, Miss Meline. If yuh want us to, we'll stay until the boys come back."

"No, I'm all right," said June. "I'm not afraid."

"Uh-huh."

McLeese went past her and entered the kitchen, where she heard him working around. Chuck Bell came over near the table and sat down in a chair. He began rolling a smoke. June was entirely disarmed. She took her hand away from the gun and picked up a magazine.

As quick as a flash Bell jerked sidewise out of his chair and secured the gun. He leered at June as he shoved the gun inside the waist-band of his overalls.

"All set, Mac," he called. McLeese came from the kitchen, glanced quickly toward the table and laughed throatily.

"That's better than knockin' her on the head," he said. "By golly, she had me worried for a minute. I don't *sabe* it yet, but that don't worry me much. Get a rope, Bell."

Bell walked back to the front door and went out, while McLeese leaned against the table and leered at June.

"Smart little lady, eh? Made a awful hit with Old Man Reber, didn't yuh? Came out here to catch Jack Silver!"

McLeese laughed scornfully. Bell came in with the rope and gave it to McLeese, who lost no time in tying June's hands and feet securely.

"Find me a handkerchief or a rag," he said. "We'd better gag her. Yuh never can tell who might come along. The road is guarded and all that, but we'll jist play safe."

Bell produced a dirty bandanna handkerchief.

"Why don'tcha find out how much she knows, Mac?" he asked.

"Whatsa use? Anyway, we've got to get goin', Chuck. Old Man Reber won't stop to ask many questions."

McLeese twisted the handkerchief, forced June's teeth apart and tied the gag. As he was finishing the job, Bell examined the gun he had taken from her. Suddenly he cried out:

"This is Jack Silver's gun!"

"What're yuh talkin' about?" asked McLeese.

"I tell yuh it is, Mac! There's the S carved on the bottom of the handle. I've seen it lots of times. Where do you suppose she got it?"

McLeese looked at June, who was none too comfortable with the gag between her teeth.

"Take that rag out and let her talk," suggested Bell, but McLeese shook his head.

"She'd lie about it, anyway."

He indicated the closed door, where June had locked Silver.

"We'll put her in there, Chuck. Grab her feet."

McLeese grasping her by the shoulders and Chuck Bell taking her feet, they carried her over to the door.

McLeese did not seem to think it strange that the hasp was fastened in place. He held June with one arm while he unfastened it. He grasped her again with both hands and kicked the door open.

And as the door flew open, something in the nature of a cyclone seemed to strike them. Jack Silver sprang from inside the room, striking Chuck Bell with his shoulder.

June's feet struck the floor heavily, and McLeese jerked away, letting her fall to the floor as Chuck Bell went spinning across the room. Jack went to his hands and knees, but was up like a flash and into the startled McLeese before he could draw a gun.

He swung a right hand at McLeese's jaw, but the blow was too high. It caught McLeese on the bridge of the nose and knocked him to his haunches against the wall. Silver turned quickly to meet the rush of Chuck Bell, and they grappled. It was evident that Bell was so dizzy from his spinning that he forgot to draw a gun; but not so McLeese. He sagged back, his broken nose painting his face with gore, and whipped out his gun and fired upward at Silver.

The report of the gun was echoed by a crash of glass, and the room was plunged in darkness. McLeese's bullet had smashed the lamp, missing Jack Silver's ear by a fraction of an inch.

Silver whirled Bell around, broke his hold and flung him toward McLeese. It was evident that Bell went down on top of McLeese, and Silver feared for the safety of June, who was only a few feet from McLeese.

He stepped in and tried to drag her out of the mêlée, but at that moment one of the men crashed into him, knocking him off his feet. He went rolling against the table, and a man fell over him. Silver struggled to his feet and met the rush of one of them.

In that darkness it was impossible for him to see which one it was. They crashed to the floor, fighting like a pair of animals, but Jack managed to tear himself away and slid along the floor.

The front door opened, and for a moment he could see the silhouette of a man, etched blackly against the moonlight.

Came the crashing report of a revolver in the room, and the silhouette sagged down heavily.

The flash of the gun had blinded Silver, and the powder smoke choked him. One of these men had shot the other, thinking it was Jack Silver. He heard this man crawling across the floor, but did not try to stop him. Then he heard him run through the kitchen, slam the door shut and go running across the yard.

Silver ran to the front door. The man who had left the house mounted his horse and spurred toward the gate. Silver turned the man over in the doorway, and the white face and staring eyes of McLeese looked up at him. He found McLeese's gun where he had dropped it on the porch, and went back in the house. He secured the lamp in the kitchen, lighted it and went into the main room.

June was still lying where they had dropped her. Silver closed the front door and came back to her. It was a simple task for him to take the gag and ropes off her and help her to a chair, where she sagged wearily. The gag had cut her lips, and there was blood on her wrists, cut by the ropes.

Silver said nothing. His face was bruised and one sleeve of his shirt was almost torn off. June stared at him, panting nervously, as he calmly rolled a cigaret with steady fingers.

"Why don't you say something?" she asked, almost hysterically.

He looked at her, a half-smile on his lips.

"I dunno," he said simply. "Don't seem to be much to say."

"Well, what is it all about? Oh, why don't you get excited? You sit there and roll a cigaret just as though nothing had happened. Who—which one did you shoot?"

"I didn't shoot," he said slowly. "Bell shot McLeese. Mebbe he thought it was me. He didn't have any cause to shoot Mac, that I know about. The door over there was too thick for me to hear much that was said, and I'm wonderin' why they had you tied up."

June shook her head. She didn't know.

"Didn't they tell yuh why?"

"Oh, I don't know what they talked about. Everything is so mixed up."

"Yeah, that's right."

He lighted his cigaret and inhaled deeply.

"It seems to me," he said smiling quietly, "that you've kinda had a hard time gettin' started on yore new job."

"Why did you have me kidnaped?" she asked.

"Me? Lord love yuh, I never did."

"I'd like to believe you, but—"

"Why should I?"

"Well, I—I—you hate Park Reber."

"Yo're not Park Reber."

"I—I work for him."

"Lotsa folks work for him, ma'am, and I never kidnaped any of them."

June bit her lip and studied Jack Silver, who looked at her frankly. He did not look like a man who would kidnap a woman. There was nothing of the sneak about him.

"What do you do for a living?" she asked bluntly.

"Trappin', mostly. I had a small herd of cattle a few years ago, but Park Reber's men killed 'em off. He didn't want me to get a start. In the winter I trap from here over into the Clear Valley side of the range. I make a good livin'."

"What do you do with the cattle you steal from Park Reber?"

It was a very blunt question. Jack Silver's eyes did not shift, but narrowed slightly, and for several moments he did not speak. Then—

"I've never stolen a cow from Park Reber."

"That doesn't check up with what I've heard, Mr. Silver."

"Probably not, ma'am, but it doesn't matter. I've eaten Diamond R beef. He killed off my cattle, didn't he? When I needed a piece of beef real bad, I took it. Reber hates me. He says he hates me because I steal his cattle, but he's a liar."

"Is it because he wants all the valley?"

"No, it's because I've got Cheyenne blood in me. You've heard his story?"

"About the Indians killing his wife?"

"Stealin' her, ma'am. Nobody knows how she died—if she did die."

"I'm sorry," said June simply.

"About my blood?" Silver smiled bitterly. "I can't help it."

He got to his feet and walked to a window and he looked out. Finally he came back and sat down.

"I don't see where your blood would make any difference," said June.

"Don't yuh? Yo're a white woman; would you marry a half-breed?"

"Why, I—I never thought of that."

"You wouldn't. Perhaps there are white women who would, but they'd not be the kind I'd want. I don't want to marry an Injun girl—so there yuh are. I'm only half good enough to marry a white woman, and I've got too much white blood to marry an Indian. Everybody hates a breed. Oh, yes they do. Even the Injuns hate a breed.

"Do yuh know what they say about a half-breed? They say he inherits the vices of both sides and the virtues of neither. Mebbe that's right."

"What about Buck Priest—did Reber steal his cattle?"

"I think so, ma'am. But this ain't lettin' us in on the secret of things. Why do yuh suppose McLeese and Bell tied you up. Who kidnapped yuh, and what was their object? I'm gettin' kinda anxious. Bell rode away, and he might come back in force. I'd hate to have yuh penned in here with me if Reber's men try to catch me. I've got my own gun and the one McLeese

31

had. If Reber found me here with you he'd hang me—especially if he found McLeese dead on the porch."

"Then you'd better go away," said June. "I can get along all right, I guess."

"I guess yuh can't. After them fellers tied yuh up and tried to lock yuh in that room? We'll find a horse to ride and I'll take yuh over to my place. At least you'll be safe over there."

June shook her head quickly.

"No, I'll stay here."

"Then I'll stay with yuh."

"And get hung for being here?"

"Mebbe. I'd sure hate myself all the rest of my life if I left yuh here alone and anythin' happened to yuh."

"Why would you care?"

"I'm half white."

"And you'd do this, even after I forced you to lead me here with a rope around your neck."

"That wasn't anythin'. You didn't pull it tight," he smiled at her and went to the front door.

"We've got to kinda make this place bull-tight," he said. "Yore name's June, ain't it? I heard it was. I'll call yuh June. It's easier to say than ma'am. My name's Jack. Prob'ly be mud before mornin'."

"Mr. Reber will come looking for me," said June.

"Yea-a-ah, and he'll find me," laughed Jack. "But I've got a hunch that Mr. Reber is goin' to have a hard time gettin' here."

"They spoke about the road being guarded. Did they mean against Mr. Reber?"

"Might be. We'll just wait and see what happens."

* * * *

Buck Priest and his men went back to the ranch and packed two horses with blankets and enough food to last them several days. It was about dark when they headed southeast toward the Porcupine hills. Priest's idea was to travel along the Porcupine for a way and then turn south toward the Circle S.

As far as he knew there had been no misbranding of cattle. Therefore he was of the opinion that the rustlers were moving a bunch of his stock toward the West Fork pass. If Park Reber were stealing cattle, that was the pass he would take them through to Clear Valley.

There was just enough moonlight to enable them to see to travel by. Buck hoped to find the rustler's camp, but after traveling far along the Porcupine he decided to head toward the Half-Wheel, which was almost due west of where they were now. He reasoned that if the rustlers knew that O'Steen had escaped wounded they would possibly drop the herd and head for the Half-Wheel.

In the meantime Park Reber had gathered a dozen riders and was also heading down the valley. Nelson had told him what the two masked men had said about the road's being dangerous, and Reber was not the man not to heed a warning. He left the road a short distance out of Tomahawk and took to the open hills where there would be no danger of an ambush.

"We'll head straight toward Jack Silver's place," he told his men. "Buck Priest is in with Silver on this deal, that's a cinch, so there's no use going to his place."

"And if it's a scheme to run a lot of cattle out of the valley they'll use the Trapper Creek pass," declared Nelson. "I'd like to notch my sight on the jasper that killed old Sam Herd."

"There'll be plenty of chances before this time tomorrow night," said Reber. "I'll clean this valley of every rustler or quit the cow business myself."

The men knew the hills well, and they were able to make good time. Reber was suffering considerably with his shoulder, but he gritted his teeth and led the way.

There were no lights showing at the Half-Wheel when Buck Priest led his men down to the road past the ranch. For quite a while they sat on their horses at a little distance from the ranchhouse, debating just what to do.

"We'll go on," decided Buck Priest. "Before daylight we can be in the West Fork pass, and if they run those cows into that pass we'll show the dirty thieves a merry time."

"Jist lemme get a sight of the fellers that leaded up O'Steen," said Rowdy. "I'm shore honin' for a chance at 'em."

"Daylight will tell the tale," said Priest. "They'll try and run 'em through early in the mornin'. I wouldn't be surprized to find the hills around the Two Bar X full of my cows."

They were about two miles south of the Half-Wheel, traveling along the road through a narrow defile in the heavy brush, when a rifle spat fire almost in front of them. It was so sudden and unexpected that the four riders whirled in a mass, trying to control their horses. From several places in the brush came orange-colored flashes, followed by the angry spat of rifle shots. Buck Priest's horse went down in a heap, pinning Buck to the ground.

Ken Mader's horse fell, but Ken flung himself free and began shooting from the ground. For several moments it was a nightmare of rearing, kicking horses and sporadic flashing of rifle and revolver shots. Mader went down on his face.

33

Rowdy's horse was shot from under him, but he managed to regain his feet and mount behind Dick Leesom and spur the frightened horse into a gallop back up the road. Dick had been shot through the side and was unable to control his horse or to shoot a gun.

A flurry of rifle shots followed them, but the bullets buzzed far over their heads.

Not one of the bushwhackers came in sight. As far as they were concerned they never existed. Buck Priest had dropped flat on his back to escape the hail of lead. His leg was pinned beneath his dead horse, and it was impossible for him to extricate it. He could see the white face of Ken Mader in the moonlight, and he cursed Park Reber and his men.

He tried to draw his leg loose from beneath the horse, but the pain forced him to desist. He was sure the leg was broken. He swore bitterly, feeling sure that they had run into the rustler's ambush.

Back in the hills, only a mile away from the road, were Park Reber and his men. They had heard the shooting, but the echoes were so confusing that none of them could tell where the shooting was taking place.

"Sounded like a battle all right," declared Reber. "We'd better head for the road, I think. Unless I'm mistaken, that's where the shooting came from."

They traveled due east, striking the road a few hundred yards north of where the ambush had been laid. They did not see Leesom and Dow, who had gone past the spot, and were heading north. But they did find Dow's hat in the road. It was a black Stetson, fairly new, but not marked with name or initial.

"Somebody goin' plenty fast," said one of the men. "That's hat's too good for a puncher to throw it away."

"No way to tell which way he was goin'," drawled a cowboy.

"We'll go south and take a chance," said Reber. And then they found Buck Priest, pinned down by his dead horse, and Ken Mader lying dead beside his dead horse. The men dismounted. Buck Priest recognized them and spat a curse at Park Reber.

"Got yuh, eh?" grunted Reber.

"Mader's dead," said one of the men.

Reber gave them orders to lift the horse off Priest's leg.

"Well, you've got me, Reber," said Priest. "My leg's busted. I hope yo're satisfied, you dirty cow thief!"

"I will be satisfied, yuh can bet on that," said Reber. "Yo're all through in this valley, Buck Priest—you and yore S\ Bar\ P outfit. When I get my hands on Jack Silver I've made a clean sweep."

"When yuh do," gritted Priest.

"Oh, I will," rasped Reber. "I've started out to clean up this valley."

"Clean! It'll never be clean as long as *you* live. You killed O'Steen today—yore men did. He saw yuh stealin' my cows. And yuh—oh what's the use? You've got the best hand, Reber. Go ahead and do what yuh want to."

"I never killed O'Steen," denied Reber.

"Yore men did."

"Did they? I didn't know it. Where's June Meline?"

"That female fiddler?"

"Yeah, that female fiddler! Where is she?"

"I heard somebody stole her."

"Oh, yuh did, eh? I reckon yuh didn't need to *hear* it. Some of you boys lift him on a horse. We'll take him along with us and settle his case at the Two Bar X."

They lifted Buck Priest to a saddle, and he cursed them for hurting his broken leg. Perhaps they were none too gentle.

"Want to rope him on, Park?" asked one of the men.

"What for? If he falls off he can't run away, can he?"

Two of the cowboys rode double and one of them led Buck Priest's horse. The jolting of the horse was misery to Priest, but he clamped his jaws tightly and held all his weight on his right stirrup.

* * * *

The first faint touch of dawn streaked the old pole corrals and the stables of the Two Bar X. Huddled in a chair beside the table in the main room sat June Meline, wrapped in a blanket, asleep. At one of the front windows stood Jack Silver. He had watched all night for the return of Bell, who he was sure would come back. The body of McLeese still lay where it fell.

He turned his head and saw June looking at him. She had slept for several hours.

"How are yuh feelin', June?" he asked.

"All right, Jack. Oh, I must have slept a long time. Why, it's morning!"

"Just about. We'll get some breakfast and then I'll rope a couple of horses. I dunno what became of my horse, but I think they took him away. We're goin' back to Tomahawk, June. Somethin' is wrong out here."

She nodded and got up from her chair.

"I'll get the breakfast, Jack. I can cook."

"I'll betcha," he smiled. "Yo're quite a woman, June. I don't blame Reber for likin' yuh. I never knew that women had the nerve you've got. After what you went through since yuh left Tomahawk yesterday, it's a wonder you've got any nerve left."

"But I've been frightened," confessed June. "If you had said 'boo!' to me yesterday I'd have dropped your gun."

"Mebbe not," said Jack smiling. "That gun is too easy on the trigger to take any chances. I might have just booed a bullet into my nervous system."

Jack laughed and turned back to the window, leaning forward tensely. There were cattle drifting past the rear of the corrals and sheds—a compact mass of moving animals heading northwest toward the West Fork pass. Jack stepped to the door and opened it enough to give him a farther view down the valley. As far as he could see down the valley there were cattle surging ahead like a brown wave.

Jack shut the door quickly. A man had slipped through the corral-fence at the corner of a shed, a man carrying a rifle in his hand.

"What is it, Jack?" asked June anxiously.

"The big steal!" he exclaimed. "I know the answer now, June. Reber's own men are stealing from him—taking a big herd over the West Fork pass. That's why they stole yuh, don't yuh see? They didn't want anybody here to see 'em. That's why there wasn't anybody here, June.

"That's why they've blocked the road against Reber. McLeese had this framed before Reber fired him. God knows how many of Reber's men are in on it. They're tryin' to send 'em over the pass before anybody can get out here to catch 'em."

"But—but they know we're here," panted June.

"They sure do," said Jack bitterly. "Keep out of line with the windows. I've got the doors fastened and I've got two guns. But our best chance is to lay low. We know too much for them to let us get out alive, June. Their plans were upset when Reber sent you out here."

"But won't they be in such a hurry to get the cattle over the pass that they'll leave us alone?"

June's answer came in the form of a bullet, which smashed out a pane of glass and thudded into the rear wall of the room. Jack drew June back against the wall, and they edged their way to the front of the room.

"Flat on the floor under the windows," said Jack. "They'll not shoot that low."

A shower of glass sprayed over them when a bullet tore through the window casing.

"Shootin' wild," said Jack easily. "Listen to the cattle."

They could hear the dull rumble of the moving herd, the soft bawling of calves.

"They're movin' a mighty big herd," said Jack. "It sure will hit Park Reber hard."

"You ought to be glad," said June wearily.

"I wonder if I am? If it was anybody but his own men I might."

"You believe in loyalty, Jack?"

"If yuh mean trustin' a friend or an employee—yes."

"You've been to school?"

Jack nodded shortly.

"Six years, June—in Cheyenne."

"Who sent you there?"

"I don't know. I don't even know who paid for it. I was sent from the reservation when I was about eight years old. I never went back there, June. I was fourteen when I came here. I worked for Buck Priest quite a while, and then I built me a place on Trapper Creek. I was goin' to be a cowman, and I had a good start, but Park Reber's men killed off my cattle. I've been in the valley eleven years."

"You are twenty-five years old, Jack?"

"I think so."

"Who was your father?"

He looked queerly at her. Another bullet smashed through the kitchen window and ricocheted off the stove.

"I don't know who he was," said Jack. He ran his fingers along the barrel of his six-shooter. "No one would tell me after I came back from school. They said I was the son of a squaw-man."

Jack sat up with his shoulders against the corner of the room. Some one had come on the porch and was near the door. Jack leaned sidewise and sent a bullet angling through the center panel. His shot was echoed by a yelp and a curse.

"They're still in there!" yelled a voice.

Bullets came through the door about two feet above the floor and more came through the smashed windows. The opposite wall of the room was beginning to show signs of wear. A bullet smashed the lamp, causing a small shower of kerosene.

Some one was trying to open the kitchen door. Jack snaked along the wall to the kitchen entrance and sent a bullet through the door just above the knob. He heard a sharp cry and turned to see June, one hand across her face. She had tried to follow him.

He rolled back to her and drew her back under the window. A bullet had come through just below the sill, and had scored her temple just enough to break the skin and raise a blue welt. She was dazed, bewildered. She tried to get to her feet, but Jack pulled her down.

"You're all right, June," he told her. "It's not serious. Stay down, girl!"

He held to her with one hand. There was smoke drifting in through the broken window—too much smoke to be caused by the shooting. Jack sniffed at it.

Wood smoke! They had fired the ranchhouse!

He could hear the flames crackling now, and the smoke was getting heavier. June was recovering, but it seemed that the injury had broken her nerve. She began crying softly and Jack patted her on the arm.

"It's all right, June," he told her. "Don't cry. You've got to hang on to yore nerve, girl. They've set the house on fire. It's do or die, I guess. We can't stay here and burn to death."

The wall was getting hot. There was a little breeze, and the seasoned old building was as dry as tinder. June blinked at him through her tears. She understood what he was saying.

"We'll crawl to the kitchen door," he told her. "I'll open the door and jump out. Mebbe I can drive 'em back so you can get away. It's our only chance. They might let yuh go and figure on catchin' yuh. I'll stop 'em as long as I can, June."

They slid along the wall to the kitchen.

The shooting had stopped. Jack knew they were merely waiting for them to try to make a break. Beside the door they stopped and Jack held out his hand to her.

"Good-by, June. You stay here until I tell yuh when to come out—if I last that long."

"Good-by, Jack." June's face was white and drawn. "I forced you into this. If it hadn't been for me you'd be free."

"Tha's all right; it was a mistake, June. It's all in the game. I reckon I'd forgive you for anythin'. Good-by."

He raised up from his haunches, grasped the door with his left hand and gave it a jerk. It stuck fast. He dropped the gun in his holster and grasped the door with both hands but it refused to open.

"Stay here, June," he panted, dropping to his knees and crawled back to the front door.

The room was full of smoke now.

He went to the door, got to his feet and tried to open it. He could force it open about two inches—enough to see that a rope ran from the knob to a porch-post.

A bullet smashed through the paneling and raked him along the forearm. He dropped to his knees, coughing from the smoke, and crawled back to June. His left forearm and hand were covered with blood.

"They've locked us in, June," he said. "If we try to get through a window they'll riddle us."

June merely stared at him, her mind refusing to work.

"You mean, we can't get out—we've got to burn?"

Jack was staring at a spot in the center of the floor. There was a metal ring sunk in the floor, and beyond it were two hinges—the roothouse trap-door.

He sprawled over and dug the ring loose. With a heave he opened the trap, and the odor of musty old vegetables filled the room. An old ladder led down to the bottom. June went down first. There was more shooting, but they could not hear the bullets now.

Jack left the trap open to give them a little light. The roothouse was about six feet deep and of about the width of the kitchen. It was cool down there, and no smoke penetrated. They took deep breaths to rid their lungs of the smoke.

On one side was an accumulation of old boxes and barrels. Jack lighted a match and almost shouted with joy. Behind those old boxes and barrels was a stairway which led to an outside roothouse door.

He flung the boxes aside, clearing the disused stairway, a prayer in his heart that the door might not be nailed down. They could hear the snapping of the flames now, the hoarse shouts of men, the crackle of guns.

Jack put his shoulder against the old slanting door and lifted enough to find that it was not fastened down.

"We'll beat 'em yet, June," he panted. "The fire seems to be mostly at the front of the house yet. We can stay here for a few minutes."

June was swaying sidewise, and before Jack could spring to her assistance she had fainted. He lifted her up and held her in his arms. In falling she had struck her head against the corner of a box, cutting it badly.

He tore the muffler from around his neck and bound it around her head. Then he picked her up in his arms and staggered up the old steps, where he hunched in as low as possible, bracing his right shoulder against the door.

* * * *

Park Reber did not lead his men straight for the Two Bar X, but took the left-hand road and headed for the Circle S, where he decided to pick up Jim Carlin and his men. He intended sending one man from there to the Lightning to get the assistance of Nort Jackson and his crew. Reber was going to have enough men to comb every inch of the country.

It was nearing daylight when they rode into the Circle S. The ranch was deserted.

"Mebbe they're chasin' rustlers already," said one of the men.

"More likely out doin' a little rustlin'," said Buck Priest grimly. His face was the color of ashes, his left leg dangling uselessly from outside the stirrup. The old man was living on his nerve now. Park Reber scowled at him, but said nothing in reply to Priest's sarcasm.

"Shall we go to the Lightnin'?" asked a cowboy.

"No," said Reber shortly, and headed for the Two Bar X.

The men were tired, sleepy, hungry; they were willing to go anywhere to stop for a while. They did not go back to the road, but cut across the hills. Daylight came swiftly, and the sun was painting the tops of the hills when they struck the road about a mile below the Two Bar X.

And here the road was a mass of cow tracks. Reber leaned forward in his saddle, pointing at them.

"The trail of the rustlers," he said. "They're headin' for the West Fork pass."

"Listen!" Nelson threw up his hand.

From far up the road they could hear the rattle of rifle shots.

"My ——!" exclaimed Reber. "The boys of the Two Bar X are tryin' to stop 'em! Come on!"

Some one lashed Buck Priest's horse across the rump with a rope, and the animal almost unseated the suffering old man. He gritted his teeth and rode along with them. The men were riding with rifles in their hands now.

About three hundred yards short of the Two Bar X, the road topped an elevation around the point of a hill and, as they swung around this point, Park Reber, riding at the head of his men, drew rein.

The whole front end of the ranchhouse was enveloped in flames, and beyond the burning house the hills were full of cattle. They saw a man running away from the corrals. He mounted a horse and headed for the cattle.

A rifle bullet struck the ground in front of Reber's horse and buzzed angrily away. The riders separated like a covey of quail. Another bullet thudded against a horse, and its rider flung himself free as the horse reared up and fell backward.

Cowboys were dismounting as swiftly as possible, letting their horses go; then they ran ahead, taking advantage of every bit of cover. Rifles began to crack as the Reber men searched the corrals and sheds with bullets.

Mounted men began riding from behind the stable, heading toward the cattle.

"Get yore horses!" yelled Reber. "They're headin' for the pass."

The men continued to shoot at the retreating cowboys. One of them pitched sidewise off his horse, and his horse came back toward the stable. Reber's men mounted swiftly and swept down on the ranch.

A man ran from the stable-door, trying to get around the corner, but a hail of bullets cut him down. He went flat on his side, rolled over and fired one shot in return. Park Reber jerked back in his saddle and slid to the ground.

At that same moment one of the men yelled warningly. The outside roothouse door was flung open and out came Jack Silver, carrying June Meline across one arm. He staggered, flung up his right hand to shoot at them, but tripped over an old water-bucket and fell flat.

Several cowboys threw themselves upon him before he could get up, and held him tightly. They yanked him to his feet, and others took charge of June.

"Well, yuh got me, I guess," panted Jack.

"I guess we have!" snorted a cowboy. "Yo're all through, you dirty half-breed."

Jack shut his lips tightly.

"Reber's been hit hard," said one of the men. "That feller down at the stable got him."

They led Jack around to where Reber was lying. But Jack paid no attention to Reber; he was staring at old Buck Priest, who was barely able to sit in his saddle.

Park Reber had the men lift him to a sitting position. He looked at Jack Silver closely.

"I swore I'd get you, Silver," he said. "I started out last night to clean out the valley. I don't know how badly I'm hurt, but it's bad enough. But you've stolen your last cow, kidnaped your last woman. If you've got any prayers to say you better say 'em."

"I'm not prayin'," said Jack coldly. "I never stole yore cows and I never kidnaped any woman."

"What else could yuh say?" cried Reber, and then to his men, "Run a rope over the ridge-pole of the stable."

The men hurried to do his bidding. Old Buck Priest had heard Reber's order, and it seemed to amuse him greatly.

"Goin' to hang the lad, eh?" he laughed. "Ha-ha-ha-ha-ha! That's good! Goin' to die with that on yore dirty soul, eh? It's like yuh, Reber."

He turned to Jack, who was being held by two men.

"Reber's men bushwhacked me last night, Jack. They killed Ken Mader. Yesterday afternoon they killed O'Steen."

"You lie!" declared Reber weakly. "You're tryin' to turn it around. You stole my cattle and my men caught yuh."

"And yore men shot Sam Herd yesterday, Priest," declared Nelson.

"Lies!" panted Buck. "All lies! We didn't know Herd was dead until we met yuh at the forks of the road, Nelson."

"The rope's ready, Park," called one of the men.

One of the cowboys threw a noose around Jack's neck, but he did not quiver. He was probably the coolest man in the crowd.

"Have you said yore prayer?" asked Reber.

Jack shut his lips tightly.

"All right," said Reber weakly.

"I wish you'd wait until June Meline recovers," said Jack. "She might have somethin' to say."

"Your time is up, Silver."

"Yuh better not hang him," said Buck Priest. "You'll be sorry, Reber. Ain't there nothin' that can save him?"

"Not a thing, Priest."

"All right, Reber. Go ahead and hang him. Ha-ha-ha-ha-ha! Hang him, you dirty old pup! Hang yore own son, and be —— to yuh! Ha-ha-ha-ha-ha!"

In spite of his weakness, Reber jerked forward, staring at Buck Priest. Jack Silver stumbled forward, his eyes on the curiously twisted features of the old cattleman. Reber tore his gaze away and looked at Jack Silver.

"You lie, Priest!" he said.

"I don't lie! He's your son, Park. His mother died when he was born and he was nursed by a squaw. Ask him who his father was—he don't know, I tell yuh!"

Jack shook his head.

"I kept track of him, Park," said Priest. "I shipped him to school and paid for it. I wanted an ace in the hole. You've always wondered if there was a child. Look at him, Reber. He's yore own flesh and blood—and you're goin' to hang him! Let's get it over with, Reber. I want to see you hang yore own son."

Reber shut his eyes, and after a few moments the tears trickled down his cheeks. The wound was sapping his strength. It was a long way to a doctor, and he knew he couldn't live till one came.

One of his men came bustling into the crowd.

"Hey," he shouted, "that fellow down by the stable is Bell, of this ranch, and the one on the hill up there is Bob Cliff, of the Lightnin'! What does it mean?"

"It means that Reber's own men planned to clean him out," said Jack Silver. "They kidnaped June Meline. I found her and brought her here. Last night Bell killed McLeese. He was on the porch and he's burned up by this time. I think you'll find that the Circle X, Lightnin' and Two Bar X outfits were makin' a big steal, but circumstances blocked 'em."

Reber opened his eyes and stared at Jack.

"Is that all true, Jack?" he asked.

"The girl's awake," burst in one of the men.

They brought her over to Reber. She saw the rope around Jack's neck.

"He—he saved me!" she said hoarsely to Reber. "Jack Silver wasn't to blame. It was your own men. Oh, you've been hurt again!"

Reber leaned back and his face was very white now.

"Come in close, boys," he said weakly. "Listen to what I'm sayin'. No time to write. Jack Silver is my son. Everything I own belongs to him. I think Buck Priest taught him to hate me. I—I didn't kill off his herd of cattle. Mebbe my men did it. But it's all right now. He owns this valley and everything else I have.

"Get Buck Priest to a doctor. I don't hate him any more. He gave me back my son. Jack—come closer. This—is—June. She's—fine. I—I—"

His head fell forward on his chest.

* * * *

There was little left of the old ranchhouse when Jack Silver and June Meline stood beside the body of Park Reber, who seemed to be smiling in his sleep. Nelson came up to Jack and held out his hand.

"You'll have to hire new crews, Jack," he said. "I imagine a lot of Diamond R men went over the West Fork pass this mornin'."

"Let 'em go," said Jack. "There's been enough killin'."

He put his good arm around June and they went down toward the stables, where the men were rigging a stretcher to carry Buck Priest back to his ranch.